Tiny and the Big Wave

Story by Annette Smith
Illustrations by Julian Bruère

Mom and Dad and Matt went for a walk with Tiny.

Tiny ran all the way down to the beach.

"Tiny!" shouted Matt.
"Come back!
Here is your leash."

Tiny ran after the seagulls.
"Woof!" she said. "Woof!"

Away went the seagulls.

Tiny ran up and down.

She ran into the water after the seagulls.

"Tiny!" shouted Dad.
"Come back here!"

A big wave came up the beach.

"Oh, **no!**" cried Matt. "Where is Tiny?"

Dad ran into the waves
to look for Tiny.

"Stay here with me, Matt,"
said Mom.

Matt looked at the big waves
and he cried.

"I can see Tiny!" shouted Dad.

He went out to get her.

"Here she is, Matt," he said.

"Tiny is safe."

"I'm all wet," said Dad.

"I'm going home."

"And I'm wet, too," said Matt.

"Come on," said Mom.

"Here is Tiny's leash."

Tiny walked home with her leash on.

"Good dog, Tiny," said Matt.